Hello, Family Members,

Learning to read is one of the most important accomplishments of early childhood. **Hello Reader!** books are designed to help children become skilled readers who like to read. Beginning readers learn to read by remembering frequently used words like "the," "is," and "and"; by using phonics skills to decode new words; and by interpreting picture and text clues. These books provide both the stories children enjoy and the structure they need to read fluently and independently. Here are suggestions for helping your child *before*, *during*, and *after* reading:

Before

- Look at the cover and pictures and have your child predict what the story is about.
- Read the story to your child.
- Encourage your child to chime in with familiar words and phrases.
- Echo read with your child by reading a line first and having your child read it after you do.

During

- Have your child think about a word he or she does not recognize right away. Provide hints such as "Let's see if we know the sounds" and "Have we read other words like this one?"
- Encourage your child to use phonics skills to sound out new words.
- Provide the word for your child when more assistance is needed so that he or she does not struggle and the experience of reading with you is a positive one.
- Encourage your child to have fun by reading with a lot of expression . . . like an actor!

After

- Have your child keep lists of interesting and favorite words.
- Encourage your child to read the books over and over again. Have him or her read to brothers, sisters, grandparents, and even teddy bears. Repeated readings develop confidence in young readers.
- Talk about the stories. Ask and answer questions. Share ideas about the funniest and most interesting characters and events in the stories.

I do hope that you and your child enjoy this book.

—Francie Alexander
Reading Specialist,
Scholastic's Learning Ventures

D0387968

For Erica Rose DiPietro
— *J.H.*

To David and Celine
— *J.K.*

Text copyright © 2000 by Joan Holub.
Illustrations copyright © 2000 by Jane Kurisu.
All rights reserved. Published by Scholastic Inc.
SCHOLASTIC, HELLO READER, CARTWHEEL BOOKS
and associated logos are trademarks
and/or registered trademarks of Scholastic Inc.

Library of Congress Cataloging-in-Publication Data

Holub, Joan.
    Backwards Day / by Joan Holub ; illustrated by Jane Kurisu.
       p.   cm.— (Hello reader! Level 3)
    "Cartwheel Books."
    Summary: Everything in school is reversed on backwards day, from reading books back to front to saying "no" instead of "yes."
    ISBN 0-439-12964-8
    [1. Schools Fiction. 2. Stories in rhyme.]   I. Kurisu, Jane, ill.   II. Title.   III. Series.
PZ8.3.H74Bac   2000
[E] — dc21   99-31961
                                                              CIP
                                                               AC

10 9 8 7 6 5 4 3   00 01 02 03 04

Printed in the U.S.A.   24
First printing, March 2000

Backwards Day

by Joan Holub
Illustrated by Jane Kurisu

Hello Reader! — Level 3

SCHOLASTIC INC.
New York Toronto London Auckland Sydney
Mexico City New Delhi Hong Kong

When we go to school
on Backwards Day,
we do everything
the backwards way!

We wear our clothes
turned willy-nilly,
inside out, flip-flopped—
How silly!

Instead of "Good morning,"
we say, "Good night."

We even sit backwards.
What a sight!

We say our letters
from Z to A.

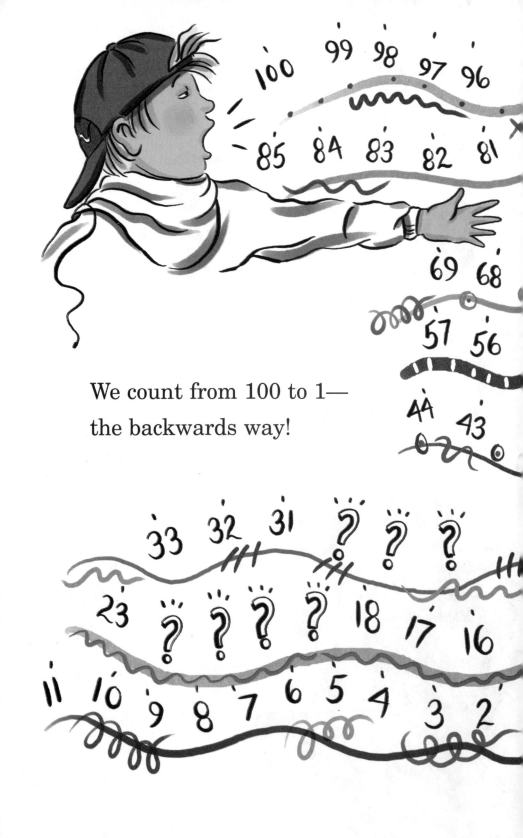

We count from 100 to 1—
the backwards way!

95 94 ? ? 91 90 89 88 87 86

? ? ? ? ? ? 74 73 72 71 70

67 66 65 ? ? ? ? 60 59 58

55 ? ? ? ? 50 49 48 47 46 45

42 41 40 39 ? ? ? ? ?

27 26 25 24

15 14 13 12

1 !!

Reading our books
is lots of fun.
We start on the last page
and end on page one.

Backwards is how
we say our names.

Backwards is the way
we play our games.

We always say "No,"
when we mean "Yes."

We always say "More,"
when we want less.

Our teacher plays music
and says, "Do not dance!"
But we twist and wiggle.
We skip and prance.

We begin every song
with the last word.

Our songs are the funniest
you've ever heard.

Our principal takes tests
and gets graded, too.
She even gets homework.
But *we* never do!

Backwards Day is over now.

It's time for us to go.

As we leave, we wave and then . . .

we tell our friends "Hello!"